SPUD

Illustrations by Angela Mitson Written by Giles Reed

The Munch Bunch are a group of fruits, vegetables and nuts.

One day they ran away from the grocer's shop where they lived.

They made their new homes in and around an old, forgotten garden shed.

This is a story about Spud, one of the Munch Bunch.

Rourke Publications, Inc.
Windermere, FL   32786

C-2058

Spud is one of the Munch Bunch.

He lives in a sack. He lives right next door to his best friend, Tom Tomato.

Spud never goes out without his smartly colored cap.

Published by Rourke Publications, Inc., P.O. Box 868, Windermere, Florida 32786. Copyright © 1981 by Rourke Publications, Inc. All copyrights reserved. No part of this book may be reproduced in any form without written permission from the publisher. Printed in the United States of America.

Library of Congress Cataloging in Publication Data

Reed, Giles.
  Spud.

  SUMMARY: The Munch Bunch use Spud's old yellow scarf on the snowman they build.
  [1. Potatoes—Fiction.   2. Snow—Fiction.
3. Vegetables—Fiction.   4. Fruit—Fiction]
I. Mitson, Angela.   II. Title.
PZ7.R2514Sp   [Fic]   80-39842
ISBN 0-86625-049-2

It was Saturday.

Spud jumped out of bed at 7 o'clock.

The first thing he did was put on his cap. Then, he put on his yellow boots.

He was ready to play with his friends.

He drew back the curtains of his bedroom and looked out.

Everything outside was covered with snow!

"Hooray!" he cried. "I am going to build a snowman today."

Spud rushed down the stairs. He put on his gloves and his old, old scarf.

His scarf was full of holes.

"I wish I had a new scarf," he thought. He opened the door and ran into the snow.

Everybody was having great fun, except poor Olly Onion. He was crying. Billy Blackberry and Scruff Gooseberry were throwing snowballs at him.

Suddenly Supercool the Cucumber came whizzing down the hill. He was on his sled.

"Look out!" he cried.

He was too late.

Emma Apple did not move quickly enough. She was knocked over into the snow.

Spud thought that sledding looked too dangerous. He decided to build his snowman.

"Help me make a snowman, Tom," said Spud.

"OK, we will build the biggest snowman in the world," replied Tom.

They started to roll the snow into a big ball.

An hour passed. They had built the biggest snowman that they had ever seen.

"Phew! That was hard work," said Spud.

"Yes," answered Tom, "but we have not finished yet. We need to find him a hat and scarf."

Just then, Supercool came back with Lizzie Leek.

"I am knitting a scarf now," said Lizzie Leek. "The snowman can have this. I have nearly finished."

"And, I have one of my old hats at home. The snowman can wear that," said Supercool.

Spud was not happy. He wanted the new scarf.

"Let the snowman have my old yellow scarf.
I will have the nice, new, red one." said Spud.

"No, certainly not," said Lizzie Leek. "I made
this one for the snowman."

Tom Tomato decided to cook some hot dogs on his barbecue.

"Never mind about the scarf, Spud," said Tom. "Have one of these hot dogs. It will warm you up!"

Tom left his fire near the snowman. Lizzie Leek carried over a pot of hot milk and some cups. Spud helped to pour the hot milk.

Everybody was busy eating and drinking. They did not notice that the heat from Tom's fire was melting the snowman.

"Look!" shrieked Scruff. "Look at the snowman. It is melting!"

They all turned around to look at the poor snowman.

His body had completely disappeared. Only his head and scarf were left.

It was too late to move the fire now.

Soon the snowman had completely disappeared.

All that was left was his hat and scarf.

"I will take back my scarf now," said Lizzie Leek.

"Since you helped me with the hot milk," Lizzie said to Spud, "you can have the new, red scarf after all."

"Oh, thank you Lizzie," said Spud. "Look! It matches my cap."

By the middle of the afternoon, the sun was shining.

The snow started to melt.

"Never mind," thought Spud. "I had lots of fun today. I built my snowman."

"I got rid of my old, yellow scarf and got myself a nice, new, red one."

Acknowledgement: This story of Spud was adapted by Giles Reed from an original idea by Ray Smith.